韓素和格妮杜

Hansel and Gretel

Retold by Manju Gregory

Illustrated by Jago

Chinese translation by Sylvia Denham

Mantra

在很久以前，有一個很窮的樵夫，他與他的妻子和兩名孩子住在一起。
男孩子的名字叫韓素，他的妹妹的名字叫格妮杜。
當時各地都正在鬧饑荒。有一天晚上，那位父親對他的妻子嘆道：
「我們沒有足夠的麵包糧食。」
「聽我說，」他的妻子說，「我們將孩子帶到樹林，然後把他們留在那裏，
他們會照顧自己的。」
「但他們可能會被猛獸撕開吞噬啊！」他哭道。
「難道你想我們都一齊死嗎？」她說。那樵夫的妻子不停的說，
直至他同意爲止。

Once upon a time, long ago, there lived a poor woodcutter with his wife and two children.
The boy's name was Hansel and his sister's, Gretel. At this time a great and terrible famine
had spread throughout the land. One evening the father turned to his wife and sighed,
"There is scarcely enough bread to feed us."
"Listen to me," said his wife. "We will take the children into the wood and leave them there.
They can take care of themselves."

"But they could be torn apart by wild beasts!" he cried.
"Do you want us all to die?" she said. And the man's wife
went on and on and on, until he agreed.

兩個小孩一直醒著，坐立不安，又飢餓，又脆弱，
他們聽到每一個字，格妮杜更流下淒苦的眼淚。
「不用擔心，」韓素說，「我知道怎樣救我們。」
他踮著腳走到花園去，在月光下，小徑上光亮雪白的卵石被照耀得像銀幣一樣，
韓素將袋口放滿卵石，然後回去安慰他的妹妹。

The two children lay awake, restless and weak with hunger.
They had heard every word, and Gretel wept bitter tears.
"Don't worry," said Hansel, "I think I know how we can save ourselves."
He tiptoed out into the garden. Under the light of the moon, bright white pebbles shone like
silver coins on the pathway. Hansel filled his pockets with pebbles and returned to comfort
his sister.

第二天早上，太陽還未升起，媽媽便把韓素和格妮杜搖醒，
「起來，我們要到樹林去，給你們每人一塊麵包，但不要一次過把整塊麵包吃了。」
他們一起出發，韓素多次停下回望家園。
「你做什麼？」他的爸爸大聲叫道。
「我只是向那坐在屋頂上的小白貓揮手說再會。」
「荒謬！」他的媽媽答道，「講老實話，那是晨早的太陽照耀著煙囱。」
其實韓素沿著樹林小徑走時，一直悄悄地將卵石丟掉到地上去。

Early next morning, even before sunrise, the mother shook Hansel and Gretel awake.
"Get up, we are going into the wood. Here's a piece of bread for each of you, but don't eat it all at once."
They all set off together. Hansel stopped every now and then and looked back towards his home.
"What are you doing?" shouted his father.
"Only waving goodbye to my little white cat who sits on the roof."
"Rubbish!" replied his mother. "Speak the truth. That is the morning sun shining on the chimney pot."
Secretly Hansel was dropping white pebbles along the pathway.

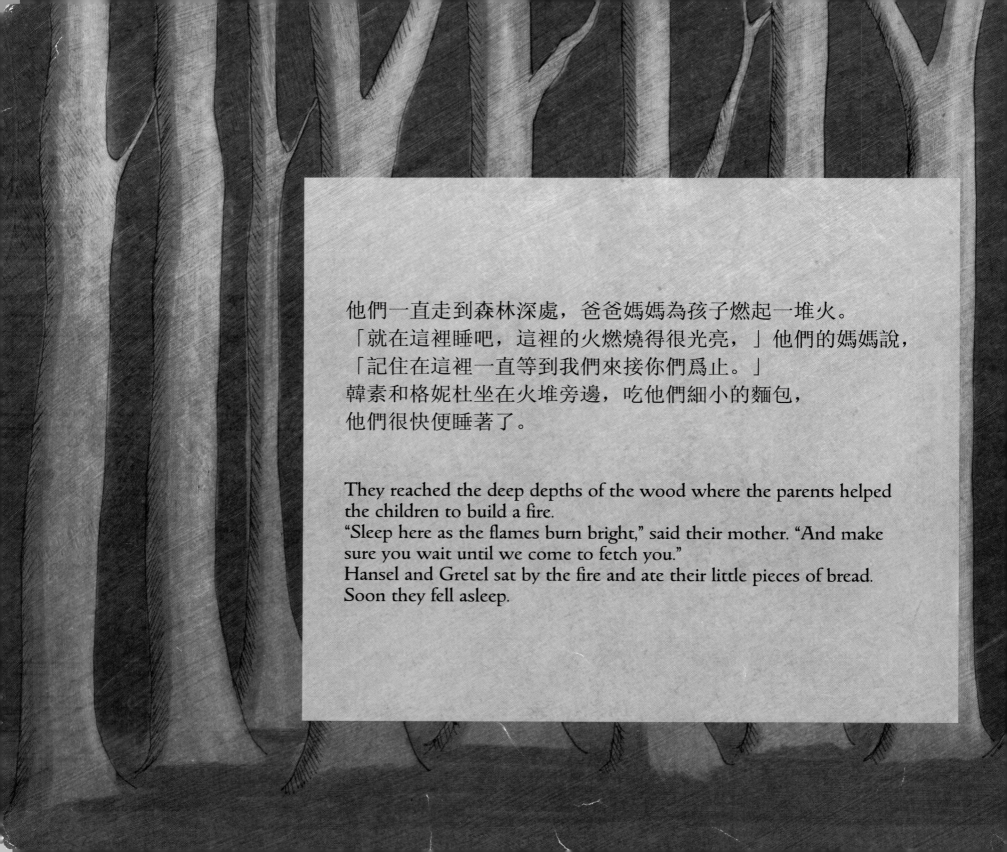

他們一直走到森林深處，爸爸媽媽為孩子燃起一堆火。
「就在這裡睡吧，這裡的火燃燒得很光亮，」他們的媽媽說，
「記住在這裡一直等到我們來接你們為止。」
韓素和格妮杜坐在火堆旁邊，吃他們細小的麵包，
他們很快便睡著了。

They reached the deep depths of the wood where the parents helped
the children to build a fire.
"Sleep here as the flames burn bright," said their mother. "And make
sure you wait until we come to fetch you."
Hansel and Gretel sat by the fire and ate their little pieces of bread.
Soon they fell asleep.

當他們醒來時，樹林已是漆黑一片。
格妮杜哭得很可憐，「我們怎樣回家啊？」
「只要等到月滿高升時，」韓素說，「我們便會見到閃耀的卵石了。」
格妮杜看著黑暗轉爲月光，她握著她哥哥的手一起走，
靠著卵石閃耀著的光覓路而行。

When they awoke the woods were pitch black.
Gretel cried miserably, "How will we get home?"
"Just wait until the full moon rises," said Hansel. "Then we will see the shiny pebbles."
Gretel watched the darkness turn to moonlight. She held her brother's hand and together
they walked, finding their way by the light of the glittering pebbles.

將近天亮時，他們便到達樵夫的小屋。
當媽媽打開門時，她大聲叫道：
「爲什麼你們在樹林睡了那麼久，
我還以爲你們不再回家了。」
她很憤怒，不過他們的爸爸卻很高興，
他根本不想把他們留下獨自離去。

過了一段時間，家中的糧食依然不足夠。
一天晚上，韓素和格妮杜聽到他們的母親說：「孩子一定要走，
我們就把他們帶到樹林更深之處，這次他們便不能再找到出路了。」
韓素悄悄地走下床，準備再去收集卵石，但這次房門卻上了鎖。
「不要哭，」他告訴格妮杜說，「我會想辦法的，睡覺吧。」

Towards morning they reached the woodcutter's cottage.
As she opened the door their mother yelled, "Why have you slept so long in the woods?
I thought you were never coming home."
She was furious, but their father was happy. He had hated leaving them all alone.

Time passed. Still there was not enough food to feed the family.
One night Hansel and Gretel overheard their mother saying, "The children must go.
We will take them further into the woods. This time they will not find their way out."
Hansel crept from his bed to collect pebbles again but this time the door was locked.
"Don't cry," he told Gretel. "I will think of something. Go to sleep now."

第二天，他們帶著更加細塊的麵包上路，孩子被帶領到他們從來未去過的森林深處。
韓素不住停下來，將麵包碎丟到地上。
爸爸和媽媽燃起火堆後便叫他們睡覺，「我們現在去砍柴，做完工作後便回來帶你們走，」媽媽說。
格妮杜與她的哥哥吃過麵包後便一直等，但始終都沒有人來。
「當月亮升起時，我們便會看到麵包碎，那時就可以尋路回家了，」韓素說。
月亮升起來，但卻見不到麵包碎，樹林的雀鳥和動物都把麵包碎吃光了。

The next day, with even smaller pieces of bread for their journey, the children were led to a place deep in the woods where they had never been before. Every now and then Hansel stopped and threw crumbs onto the ground.
Their parents lit a fire and told them to sleep. "We are going to cut wood, and will fetch you when the work is done," said their mother.
Gretel shared her bread with Hansel and they both waited and waited. But no one came.
"When the moon rises we'll see the crumbs of bread and find our way home," said Hansel.
The moon rose but the crumbs were gone.
The birds and animals of the
wood had eaten every one.

「我們很快便會在這荒野中找到出路的，」韓素說。
兩個孩子在森林中覓路，走了三日，又飢餓，又疲倦，
只是吃一些野莓充飢，最後他們就躺在一棵樹下睡著了。
他們被一隻銀白色的小鳥的美妙歌聲吵醒，
當那隻小鳥飛入森林時，他們便跟著它跑，
直至他們來到一間屋子，他們從未見過如此奇妙的屋。

"We will soon find our way out of this wilderness," said Hansel.
The children searched the woods for three days. Hungry and tired,
feeding only on berries, at last they lay down under a tree to sleep.
They were awakened by the sweet song of a silver white bird. When the
bird flew off into the forest the children followed, until they reached the
most wonderful house they had ever seen.

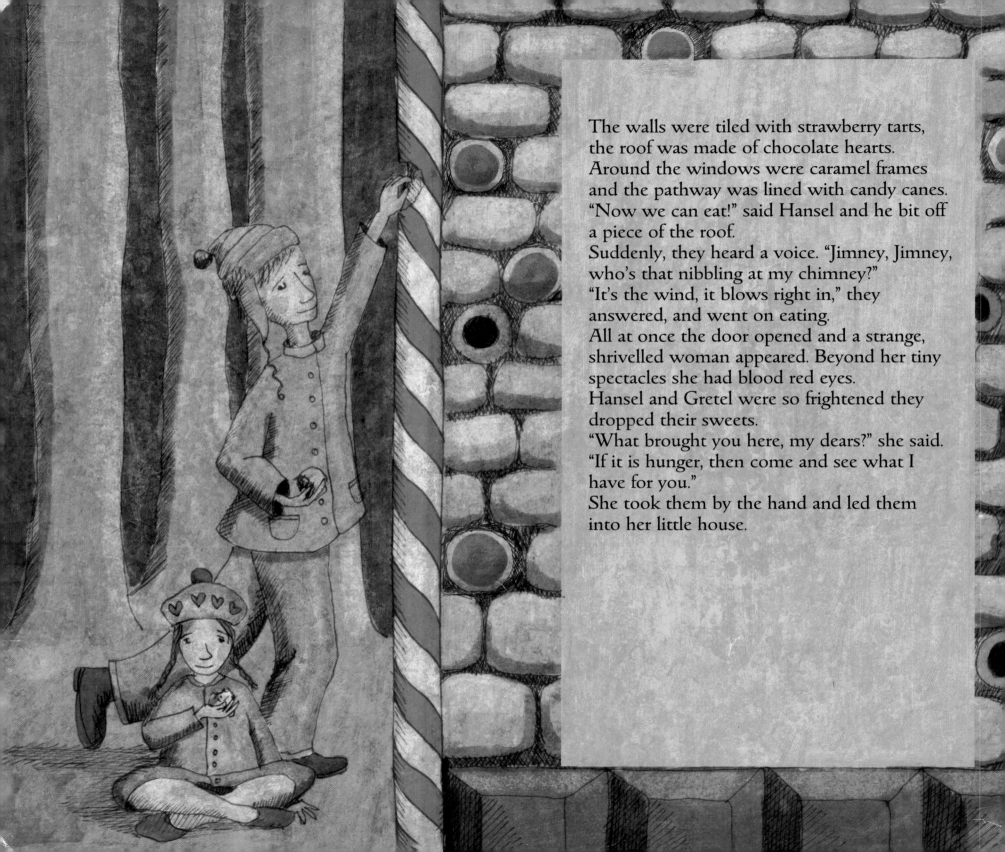

The walls were tiled with strawberry tarts,
the roof was made of chocolate hearts.
Around the windows were caramel frames
and the pathway was lined with candy canes.
"Now we can eat!" said Hansel and he bit off
a piece of the roof.
Suddenly, they heard a voice. "Jimney, Jimney,
who's that nibbling at my chimney?"
"It's the wind, it blows right in," they
answered, and went on eating.
All at once the door opened and a strange,
shrivelled woman appeared. Beyond her tiny
spectacles she had blood red eyes.
Hansel and Gretel were so frightened they
dropped their sweets.
"What brought you here, my dears?" she said.
"If it is hunger, then come and see what I
have for you."
She took them by the hand and led them
into her little house.

牆壁是用草莓餡餅堆砌而成，
屋頂是用心型巧克力造的，
窗的周圍是焦糖製造的窗框，
而小徑則有一排排的糖果棒。
「我們現在可以吃了！」韓素一邊說，
一邊咬下一塊屋頂。
突然他們聽到一個聲音，「嚴東，嚴東，
是誰在咬我的煙囱？」
「是風啊，它吹了進來，」他們答道，
並繼續吃。
屋門突然打開，一個又奇怪，
又皺萎的老婦出現，在她那細小的眼鏡後面
是一對血紅的眼睛，韓素和格尼杜害怕得連
糖果都丟了。
「是什麼把你們帶到這裡來，親愛的？」
她說，「如果是肚子餓的話，
那麼便進來看看我有什麼可以給你們吃。」
她拉著他們的手，帶他們進入她的小屋。

韓素和格妮杜獲得很多很好吃的東西！蘋果、果仁、牛奶和鋪滿蜜糖的薄餅。
跟著他們便倒睡在兩張鋪了白色床單的床，好像已經到了天堂一樣。
那個老婦盯著兩個小孩說：「你們兩個都太瘦，現在就造美妙的夢吧，
明天你們的惡夢便要開始呢！」
這位有一間可以吃的屋和視力不好的奇怪老婦只是假扮友善，
其實她是一個可惡的女巫。

Hansel and Gretel were given all good things to eat! Apples and nuts, milk, and pancakes covered in honey.
Afterwards they lay down in two little beds covered with white linen and slept as though they were in heaven.
Peering closely at them, the woman said, "You're both so thin. Dream sweet dreams for now, for tomorrow your nightmares will begin!"
The strange woman with an edible house and poor eyesight had only pretended to be friendly. Really, she was a wicked witch!

到了早上，那可怕的女巫抓住韓素，把他推入籠去，
被困和很害怕的韓素高聲求救。
格妮杜立即走過來，「你要把我的哥哥怎麼樣？」她哭著說。
那女巫一面笑一面滾動著她血紅的眼睛，
「我正要將他弄好後便吃了他，」她答道，
「你來幫我吧，小朋友。」
格妮杜嚇得魂不附體。
她被遣去女巫的廚房工作，要準備特大的食物給她的哥哥吃。
但是她的哥哥拒絕增肥。

In the morning the evil witch seized Hansel and shoved him
into a cage. Trapped and terrified he screamed for help.
Gretel came running. "What are you doing to my
brother?" she cried.
The witch laughed and rolled her blood red eyes.
"I'm getting him ready to eat," she replied. "And you're
going to help me, young child."
Gretel was horrified.
She was sent to work in the witch's kitchen where
she prepared great helpings of food for her brother.
But her brother refused to get fat.

那女巫每天都去看韓素，「伸出你的手指，」她厲聲說，
「讓我看看你有多胖！」
韓素遞出他藏在袋內的幸運叉骨，視力很差的女巫完全不
明白這男孩子為什麼會一直都這麼瘦。
三個星期之後，她再也按捺不住了，
「格妮杜，快拿木頭來，我們要將那男孩子放進鍋內，」
女巫說。

The witch visited Hansel every day. "Stick out your finger,"
she snapped. "So I can feel how plump you are!"
Hansel poked out a lucky wishbone he'd kept in his pocket.
The witch, who as you know had very poor eyesight, just
couldn't understand why the boy stayed boney thin.
After three weeks she lost her patience.
"Gretel, fetch the wood and hurry up, we're going to get
that boy in the cooking pot," said the witch.

格妮杜慢慢地推動火爐的火，那女巫忍耐不住，
「火爐應該已經準備好了，走進去，看看是否已經夠熱！」
她大聲叫道。
格妮杜其實知道女巫心中想怎樣，「我不知道怎樣進去，」她說。
「傻瓜，真蠢的孩子！」女巫奴吼道，「火爐的門已經很闊了，
連我也可以進去啊！」
為了證明她是對的，她便把頭伸了進去。
格妮杜快如閃電的將女巫的整個身體推進火爐去，
她把火爐的鐵門關上，鎖上栓，然後走去叫喊著的韓素，
「女巫已死！女巫已死！可惡的女巫就此沒命了！」

Gretel slowly stoked the fire for the wood-burning oven.
The witch became impatient. "That oven should be ready by now. Get inside and see if it's hot enough!"
she screamed.
Gretel knew exactly what the witch had in mind. "I don't know how," she said.
"Idiot, you idiot girl!" the witch ranted. "The door is wide enough, even I can get inside!"
And to prove it she stuck her head right in.
Quick as lightning, Gretel pushed the rest of the witch into the burning oven. She shut and bolted the iron
door and ran to Hansel shouting: "The witch is dead! The witch is dead! That's the end of the wicked witch!"

韓素像小鳥一樣從籠裏跳出來，

Hansel sprang from the cage like a bird in flight.

韓素和格妮杜互相擁抱，他們唱歌跳舞，歡呼著走來走去。
他們在屋子的每一個角落都找到裝滿珍珠、綠寶石、紅寶石、
以及各種珍貴物品的寶箱，
韓素和格妮杜把他們的袋口都填得滿瀉。
「我們有奇妙的珍寶，但是我們怎樣才能逃離這個野林呢？」
格妮杜嘆道。
「不用擔心，我們會一起找到返家的路途的，」韓素說。

Hansel and Gretel hugged each other. They danced and sang and ran
around with joy. In every corner they found treasure chests filled with
pearls, emeralds, rubies and all kinds of worldly precious things. Hansel
and Gretel filled their pockets to overflowing.
"We have wondrous treasures, but how do we escape from the wild
wood?" sighed Gretel.
"Don't worry, together we will find our way home," said Hansel.

經過三個小時之後，他們來到一跳河。
「我們不能過河，」韓素說，「這裡沒有船，沒有橋，只有清澈的藍色河水。」
「看！在漣漪上有一隻純白色的鴨正在游來游去，」格妮杜說，「它或者可以幫我們。」
於是他們一起唱：「有白色閃耀翅膀的白鴨啊，請你細聽，這條河又深又闊，
你能否載我們到對岸啊？」
那隻鴨子游過來，先把韓素載過去，然後再將格妮杜安全地載過河。
在河的另一邊，他們見到的是一個熟識的世界。

After three hours they came upon a stretch of water.
"We cannot cross," said Hansel. "There's no boat, no bridge, just clear blue water."
"Look! Over the ripples, a pure white duck is sailing," said Gretel. "Maybe she can help us."
Together they sang: "Little duck whose white wings glisten, please listen.
The water is deep, the water is wide, could you carry us across to the other side?"
The duck swam towards them and carried first Hansel and then Gretel safely across the water.
On the other side they met a familiar world.

他們一步一步的尋覓回到樵夫的小屋的路。
「我們到家了！」兩個孩子高聲叫道。
他們的爸爸笑容滿面，「你們走後我沒有開心過，」他說，
「我到處找你們⋯」

Step by step, they found their way back to the woodcutter's cottage.
"We're home!" the children shouted.
Their father beamed from ear to ear. "I haven't spent one happy moment since you've been gone," he said.
"I searched, everywhere..."

「媽媽呢？」
「她走了，當再沒有任何可以吃的東西時，她怒氣沖沖的走了，
說我以後不會再見到她的了，現在就只有我們三個。」
「還有我們珍貴的寶石，」韓素一面說一面伸手入袋取出一顆雪白的珍珠。
「啊！」他們的爸爸說，「我們所有的問題都似乎解決了！」

"And Mother?"
"She's gone! When there was nothing left to eat she stormed out saying I would never see
her again. Now there are just the three of us."
"And our precious gems," said Hansel as he slipped a hand into his pocket and produced a
snow white pearl.
"Well," said their father, "it seems all our problems are at an end!"